Small tales of little creatures

By James Lynch

Drawings by Ruth Mullin

To the Mutter Spirit and all who have it

Chapter One- in which we meet a family of voles and some of their neighbours

Ruth Mullin switched on the kettle. In two skips she crossed the kitchen and peered down at the little hole under the small fir tree outside the window.

She dropped a Redbush teabag into a tin cup. She liked tin cups best as they reminded her of camping trips, which were her favourite holidays.

She opened the cupboard and chose some plain oatcakes from a selection of chocolate, cheese and plain.

She crushed up the oatcakes in her hand and ran outside. She dropped the crumbs just outside the little hole.

When she got back into the kitchen the kettle was boiling. She made her cup of tea and picked up a pair of binoculars from the top of the fridge.

She sat at the table sipping her tea. She kept one hand lightly on the binoculars beside her.

After about a minute, a tiny, twitchy nose peeped out timidly from the hole, sniffing the air carefully. The nose was followed by a small, brown, hairy face. Sensitive whiskers and bright eyes checked all around for signs of danger.

Ruth picked up the binoculars and turned the wheel to focus. She saw two paws grab some oatcake and a tiny body darting back down the hole again.

A few moments later the little head reappeared. The creature was more comfortable now and he sat half out of the entrance to his burrow enjoying some crumbs. He turned the pieces of oatcake around and around in his paws as he nibbled at speed.

This small creature was a vole. A vole is an animal like a mouse but with a shorter tail. This vole was a male and his name was Eric. He and his wife Maura had been living here for some time. They had dug the burrow themselves, bit by bit under the Mullins' garden until it was large with lots of tunnels to go in and out, which is important for safety reasons.

Being prepared for emergencies had become very important to them both since they had children.

Eric liked to say that they lived at No-1 Abies Koreana Forma Chlorocarpea. He didn't know what that meant but it was written on a tag half way up the small fir tree which shaded the main entrance to their burrow and he liked the sound of it. It sounded interesting and important.

Eric brought some crumbs down into the burrow for the family. Maura was slightly smaller than him and she had freckles. Actually, freckles are very difficult to see on the small hairy nose of a vole but she insisted they were there and Eric never disagreed as he thought he could probably see them too and it made her happy when he did.

Eric and Maura had five children: Anna, Sara, Laura, Jamie and Carla.

Vole babies are born in a very tumbling, rolling altogether sort of a way so that it would be hard for us to tell who came out first, second, last or together but voles themselves know just as well as we do, who is the oldest or youngest in the family. Anna and Sara were twins – which even for other voles was hard to explain, but they had decided from their first day that that was what they were and so that was that.

Today was a big day in the burrow because the children would be let out on their own for the first time.

Eric gathered the whole family together. Everybody was given some oatcake to nibble on, as voles concentrate far better when they have some little thing to munch.

Eric cleared his throat and began to speak in his deepest, most serious voice. Every young vole hears this speech from their parents. Eric had heard it from his own Dad.

"It has been said that the world is a hard place for little things and we are some of the littlest things there are. But we are not helpless. No, we are clever and when we need to be we are brave. We have family. We help and support each other in all things. Our needs are simple and we have the Vole Code to live by."

There are only five parts to the vole code as voles have fairly small memories.

"You must learn and remember the sacred tenets of the Vole Code," Eric continued, "repeat after me, children."

1- Respect all animals and plants. Respect yourself.
2- Never forget to look up for danger.
3- Always enjoy food and never miss a meal.
4- Always keep your fur clean and well groomed.
5- Never leave the house without your emergency whistle.

The whole family repeated the code several times.

The vole emergency whistles were hanging in a row of seven pegs by the main entrance to the burrow. When a vole goes out it will put one of these whistles into its fur. It is to be blown in case of emergency. It is extremely high-pitched. Not even a dog could hear it but it alerts all the voles in the area that help is needed and danger is about.

Maura was nervous. She kept checking and rechecking that all her children's fur was perfectly clean and in place. She handed a whistle to each child in turn and kissed them on the ear.

"Be alert, be careful, have fun and don't forget to eat," she said, handing each of them some food from the store at the back of the burrow.

The children themselves were nervous as they scrambled up the tunnel to the entrance. The whole world got brighter than they had ever seen before.

Anna and Sara led the way and made sure to look confident and brave for the others. One by one they came out into the world for the first time. They looked up and kept a paw near their emergency whistles at first. Birds of prey like red kites, buzzards, owls and crows, magpies, jackdaws and jays, are always on the lookout for a vole to grab and to gobble up for dinner.

In the burrow, Maura was cleaning her ears. This is something which makes voles feel a lot calmer and they can often be seen doing it when they feel upset.

The feeling a vole has the first time they leave the burrow is one they never forget. It is a better feeling perhaps even than learning to ride a bicycle. The sun warms their fur and the grass tickles the soft pads on their paws. The world is so much bigger than they imagined. And they do imagine; they talk about it down in the burrow when they are as small as a button.

These five vole children were jumping and rolling in the grass; they stopped often to look around and look upward for danger though.

"What's this?" said Anna, pointing at a broken snail shell. All the children gathered round.

If you look closely at a snail shell you will notice that it is beautifully designed with patterns of circles within circles in browns and blacks and greys.

The voles looked and sniffed.

"Oh," said Jamie, "it's lovely." "Not sure about the taste though," he continued, having a little nibble.

"Perhaps we should bring a sample home for Mum and Dad to explain," said Sara.

"Look there," said Laura, "there's another one."

Just a little way away there was another snail shell and beyond that another and beyond that again. It seemed that there was a trail of broken snail shells heading off across the field.

"Let's follow the trail," said Laura.

"Should we, do you think?" said Anna and Sara to each other. As the oldest and twins they felt responsible for everyone's safety.

"Come on," said Laura "it'll be an adventure."

"Well......" said Jamie, nibbling on a piece of grass to help him decide.

"Ok let's," said Carla who was the youngest and smallest and always tried to be as brave as the older ones.

"Ok, we'll go," said Sara, "but be careful."

"Check your whistles," said Anna.

So they followed the trail, one shell at a time. After a short time, they heard a voice.

It was singing. It was a beautiful song, sweet and clear so that it lifted their hearts and spirits.

They followed the sound and saw a brown, speckled bird. His head was thrown back and he was singing proudly.

All the voles stopped in their tracks. Was this a bird of prey or a crow? They thought back to the lessons they had had back in the burrow on the subject of bird dangers.

Birds of prey have large, hooked beaks and powerful claws. Crows have piercing eyes, long, strong beaks, and, crows are not brown. This bird should be safe.

"Hello," called Laura, "hello!"

The bird stopped in mid note and shook its head.

"What, what," he shouted, "what's this?"

The little voles shrunk back a little.

"Well speak UP," said the bird.

"Please," said Sara, "we were wondering just what sort of a bird you might be.....please." Voles are very polite and extra polite when they are a little nervous.

"What kind of bird, what kind of bird indeed. You must be a very, very know-nothing kind of a little mouse type thing indeed, indeed. I am a song thrush, only the greatest singer in the world, I'll have you know. My name is Eugene - are you sure you're never heard of me. I'm quite famous you know."

Sara and Anna said they were sorry but they didn't know him. They complimented him on his wonderful song. Each of the voles introduced themselves except Carla who was feeling very frightened and shy and wanted very much to groom her ears just then.

"Ah," said Eugene, poking a long wing feather in Carla's direction, "so you're the quiet one of the bunch eh. Not me, no. No good. You must speak up, you must sing out. I'm the best at that you know, the best."

And he burst into song again.

Suddenly, there was a flapping of feathers and a loud cry of "Rubbish" and another bird appeared.

"Hello," he said, "I'm Charles, a blackbird. Has this old windbag been telling you tall tales? If you want to hear the very best singer in the world you must listen to me!"

With that Charles began to sing. Then Eugene began to sing. They both sang at the tops of their voices. They sang higher and higher, louder and louder trying to outdo each other. They sang and trilled and tweeted as if their very lives were at stake.

"Oh," said Jamie, "when they sing like that it's really quite an awful noise." And it was.

"Let's go home."

So they followed the trail of snail shells home. Jamie even kept one as a souvenir.

That night all the vole children slept very well indeed, except for little Carla. She was upset. She couldn't forget Eugene calling her "the Quiet One". She didn't want to be "the Quiet One". She had just as much to say as anyone else really and she didn't like being told what she was like. She thought she should do something, or think something, about it. She wanted to figure the whole thing out.

The sun was still rising next morning when Carla left the burrow. Everyone else was sound asleep but she had slept very little. She cleaned her ears and fur as quickly and quietly as she could and crept out the nearest tunnel.

The grass was still cold and wet with dew when she came out. She told herself that was the reason for the shiver that ran down her back but it's a very unusual and frightening thing for a young vole to go out all alone as she was.

She started to walk and think. She wanted to think out the problems of how people thought about each other and talked about each other and spoke to each other.

After a while she needed to have a sit down and use all of her energy for thinking because it turned out that these problems were very knotty and difficult problems indeed. She sat on a stone and started rubbing her chin with her paw. She had seen her father do this when he was thinking about something important and she figured that this might help. She also tried to make her brow all full of lines as she had seen happening when her parents were thinking out something serious.

As she was sitting and thinking she saw something flash from behind a rock and into a patch of grass. A moment later the shape flashed out again and back behind the rock. It really was moving very quickly, but it seemed to be shaped a little like a vole.

It zoomed by again, back into the grass.

The next time it went by Carla said: "Excuse me." She thought that the blur was slightly less blurry for a moment but it didn't stop.

The next time the creature moved she spoke louder: "Hello, who are you please?"

The blur came to a sudden halt.

"The question is," it said, "can YOU see ME? Or rather HOW can you see me?"

The speaker was a creature very much like a vole but with a very long nose.

"I am Sebastian, the shrew, master of disguise and camouflage," he announced. "I am practically invisible, if I choose to be. Are you sure you can see me?"

"Yes," answered Carla. "Sorry," she added, not wanting to be rude.

"Well," said Sebastian, looking a little crest-fallen, "this is strange."

"Although," he perked up, "you must have very good eye-sight indeed. That's it. You must have most incredible, amazing eyesight. You see I am a shrew and we shrews are skilled in the arts of moving without being seen.

 We learn from a young age all about camouflage, mis-direction of the eye, moving without a sound and many things a little vole like yourself would not understand. We blend into the environment so that we can retrieve food in the open and move about by day free from attack. You're sure you can......."

 Carla nodded.

 Just then a shadow came over them from above. Carla and Sebastian both looked up.

 Carla's paw went to find her whistle but it wasn't there!

 At the same time back in the burrow the day was just beginning. As usual, Maura checked all the children and woke them with a bit of a groom. Anna and Sara were curled up in a little ball together. Laura was already up and wanting to get out. Jamie was asleep on what looked like a broken snail shell.

 But where was Carla?

 Maura went and woke Eric, who was inclined to sleep later as he got older and told him that Carla was missing. Together they organised a search of the burrow, which was really quite large. All the other children were sent to check every nook and cranny of their underground home. They went about calling for their youngest sister but found no one and got no reply.

 Outside Carla had realised that she had forgotten to take her emergency whistle with her.

"I must disappear," said Sebastian and he ran away. Carla could clearly see him running away. He was very fast but not invisible.

Another dark shadow flew over her. Carla looked up and her eyes searched the sky for danger.

Up there she didn't see a buzzard or a jay as she had feared, but something amazing.

She saw a group of small black and white birds flying faster and more acrobatically than she could have imagined possible. They were sharp and speedy; darting up and down, looping the loop and most amazingly of all, skimming the ground so close that it seemed they had to crash, but they never did.

Carla stood on the tips of her tippy-toes and stared at the aerial display with her mouth wide open.

"Wow," she said to herself, "how wonderful."

The birds she was watching were house martins. They had made their nest under the eaves of Ruth Mullin's house and they were busy chasing insects to bring home to feed their hungry chicks.

As Carla watched them one of them alighted on a nearby clothesline. She saw the little vole looking to the sky, twisting and turning her head to watch the martins.

"Hello small animal," she called down, "should you be out on your own at your age?"

"Probably not but I needed to do some thinking."

"When you have worries, little one, the best thing to do is flying, not thinking. The wind blows all your cares clean out of your head. "

"I can't fly." "I can dig though."

"Hold up your paws."

With that the house martin swooped down and caught a hold of both Carla's paws and in a split second she was lifted into the air and with a ZOOM and a WHOOSH, she was flying.

Back in the burrow the search party was reporting that there was no sign of Carla. Maura was doing one last check when she found a little note.

"Look," she said, "it's from Carla."

She read it out loud: "I've gone for a walk to do some thinking – Carla."

"Right," said Maura, "let's go find her."

As they marched out the main entrance and each picked up their whistle, they realised that Carla's was still there. Now they were really worried.

Now, this would be a good time to mention that House Martins are not actually as good at flying as they might seem but they are very fast and very brave and they love to fly.

You can make wonderful things happen when you do something you love.

Carla was finding this out. She felt terrified and excited all at the same time.

"Oh myyyyyyyy," she screamed as she rocketed upwards into the air. Everything was moving so fast! The wind was pinning her ears back against the sides of her head. Her tummy was doing handstands and cartwheels.

"Don't worry," said the house martin, "I've got a good hold of you. You'll be absolutely fine. Sheila is my name by the way, what's yours?"

"Carla," said Carla, "please be careful."

"There's no need to be careful when you fly," replied Sheila, "when you fly you should be happy."

Sheila was still holding Carla by the wrists and Carla was holding on very tightly to Sheila by the ankles. Sheila was putting on a display of daredevil flying to be proud of.

Down below the rest of the vole family were searching for Carla. It was Jamie, who having stopped to nibble a little food, looked up and noticed something very strange going on. Was that a little vole hanging from under that speeding, crazy bird? Could that be Carla? He blew his whistle as loudly as he could.

By now Carla was enjoying the flight. She particularly liked it when they came close to the ground and she had to lift her legs up to stop them brushing against the grass.

When they were that close to the earth she could look down

at the ground rushing by underneath her and really understand how very, very fast they were going.

"Yippee," she said, as they dipped over the roof of a shed.

Below her, all the vole family were blowing their whistles.

"What's that bird doing to my daughter," said Eric.

Carla heard the whistles and looked down.

"Oh, my family are down there Sheila and they are worried. May I get down again now please?"

"The thing about that," said Sheila, "is, we house martins don't really land on the ground very often. Only to drink and bathe really. Don't worry though, I'll fly in very, very low and I'll slow as much as I can and you will have to let go and run at the same time. That way we should be ok, I think."

Carla didn't like the sound of that "I think" and she didn't like the sound of being dropped at all but she was also feeling brave now and she knew she would have to do it.

"Ok Sheila, let's try."

The voles on the ground were watching and worrying.

"It's not a dangerous bird," Eric was explaining, "I believe it is a house martin."

"But what are they doing?" said Maura.

"I think they are coming in to land."

"Ok," said Sheila, "we are coming in to land. Get ready.

When I say "Start", start your back legs running.

When I say "Now", Let Go.

When you touch the ground, try to keep running. Here we goooo!"

Carla took a deep breath and got ready. The ground was zooming up towards her so fast it nearly made her head spin.

She concentrated hard.

"START!"

Carla started her little back legs running as fast as she could make them go. They flew lower till they were nearly touching the ground.

Maura wanted to cover her eyes but she didn't, she wanted to wish her youngest safely down.

"NOW," Sheila shouted. Carla worked her legs as hard as she could and closed her eyes. Then she let go....

She hit the ground in a rolling, tumbling ball that travelled a long way and then bumped to a halt in a flowerbed. Carla unrolled and sneezed some dirt from her nose.

"Hooray," she said, realising she was fine. "Thank you Sheila."

"Any time," said Sheila, doing a loop the loop in the sky.

The next thing Carla knew she was being hugged by her family. Her mother removed a flower petal from her head and gave her a little groom. Everybody wanted to know what had happened and what it was like to fly. Carla told them the story in detail and they all listened in silence.

Her mother and father did have a talk with her later. They reminded her of the dangers of going out alone and of not carrying your emergency whistle with you at all times when you go outside. Carla apologised for worrying everyone, but they said that they were so pleased to find her safe that they were not really angry.

Before bed that night Maura called Carla over and said: "By the way, what was it that you wanted to think about Darling, what was on your mind?"

"Oh it's really ok now," said Carla, "it's not so important".

After her exciting day, Carla knew that it didn't really matter what other people said you were. She knew that she was brave and she could talk as well as anyone. She wasn't "the quiet one" or anything else. She was Carla and she was very tired.

She slept very well indeed.

Chapter two- in which the vole family face great danger of two different kinds

It was a terrible storm.

It rained for two whole days and nights. The wind howled. Black rain fell hard from a dull grey sky. The rain was so heavy, the wind was so strong and the air was so cold that Ruth Mullin was trapped in her house. At night the wind was so strong that sometimes it sounded like a great, angry animal that might smash in the windows.

Ruth tried to be brave but sometimes she was a little frightened.

She looked out the window at breakfast and saw the small trees in the garden bent under the power of the wind. A crow was chasing and attacking a red kite high above and the rain kept on raining.

Branches of trees had been broken off by the force of the storm and lay in the garden and in the fields and on the roads.

Blankets of soaked and sad looking leaves lay all around.

All the while the storm seemed to be trying to get into Ruth's house. The wind was pulling at the windows and the door; the rain was looking for any tiny hole to leak into.

This was hard, hard weather for all the animals that burrow or nest. Foxes, badgers, weasels, stoats, mice and voles and all kinds of burrowing things were curled up underground waiting and hoping for the storm to pass. The chicks of birds were huddled in their nests hoping their little homes were strong enough to last out the wind and the rain.

It was a bad time for the animals. A lean time. The hunting animals found it hard to get food at times like this and they and their children would soon be hungry.

In their burrow under the Mullins' garden Eric and Maura were doing all they could to keep their family safe and to calm their fears.

They had a store of food so that they did not need to go out to keep them from hunger. But the wind blew into their home and chilled their little bodies and the sound of thunder and the roar of the wind sounded to the vole children like a hungry beast outside.

Eric and Maura made sure to keep the children nibbling on tasty treats to help them stay not too frightened. They also told them stories to take their minds off the fearful weather.

Just like us all the animals have their own folk tales; stories that are the memory of that species, like a vast collection of the thoughts and feelings of that type of creature over thousands of years. The type of stories they tell will tell you a lot about what is most important to that kind of animal. Fox stories will often be about hunting, thrush stories will be about singing contests. The stories of the house martins will be about the greatest flyers.....

The stories of voles are often about daring escapes from danger or great feasts that last a whole week.

Sometimes these stories answer important questions about how certain things came to be as they are. When a curious leveret (that's a young hare) asks why it has such very long legs and why its black tipped ears are so very, very long, its parents will have an old story to tell that will explain just how and why those things came to be.

Eric was telling one of the oldest and best loved of all the vole sagas - the story of how voles got their small tails:

"Now sometimes you'll meet a mouse (a wood mouse or a field mouse or a house mouse, for instance) or even a rat (in which case you should really be running away) and they might make fun of your short tail and make much of their own long tails. This should not make you feel small or sad; although it is impressive the practical uses a mouse or a rat can put their tail to; and it will not make you sad so long as you know the true and real story of how voles came to have their short tails. Once you know this story you will be very proud of the tail you have.

I need to take you all the way back, through many, many generations of voles to nearly the very beginning of the vole folk.

Close your eyes and travel back in your imagination.

Those were hard times; hard and wild and tough and in those times voles had long tails.

Keep your eyes tight shut and try to imagine having a big, long tail.

Strange, isn't it? But it's true. We had them many, many generations ago.

Back then, times were so lean that all the voles had to live together and share their food. That's every vole from every vole family from everywhere, all together in one enormous burrow. That way they could share the food out evenly, and even though everyone was a little hungry, no one went entirely without."

Jamie never liked this part of the story. Even though he had heard it many times it always made him very sad to think of all those voles without plenty to munch on. His tummy made a little rumbling sound and he nibbled extra hard on the seeds he was eating.

"We all know the phrase "many whistles make more safety" and of course there is a lot of sense in that. But, it is also true that when you bring everybody and all the food together in one place at the same time; when all the animals are hungry and hard up; the word will get around to some of the dangerous creatures and the clever creatures that there is a large store of food to be had, and even voles to be gobbled, all neatly and nicely put together for the taking.

The rats, weasels and stoats were hungry too and so it wasn't long before the trouble started.

All the voles together of course could defend the burrow from an individual weasel or a couple of rats but it was the stoats, those cunning devils, who organised. They got together and planned, and they elected a general, a great ugly brute called Scar, and they attacked in force under cover of night.

That was a bad time to be a vole. Their own giant burrow was no longer a place of safety, but a trap. The stoats blocked every tunnel, leaving no way out for any vole.

As the stoats advanced it seemed that all was lost, it looked like the end of voles for good. The stoats were hungry and angry and ready to gobble up not only the food, but the vole folk as well. We all remember this as the darkest hour in the history of our kind.

It was then that a very tiny and weak vole called Richard stepped forward. He challenged Scar himself to a duel. If he won the stoats were to leave the burrow and never attack it again. If he lost, well, all was lost.

There was no reason for Scar to accept the challenge of this small and weak little thing. In fact the idea was laughable and Scar did indeed laugh, a big booming laugh that made poor Richard even more afraid than he already was.

But Scar was the general of all the stoats, the toughest and the roughest of them all. He was covered from the tip of his nose to the tip of his tail in the many battle scars that gave him his name; how would it look if he refused a challenge from this weakling? Perhaps the other stoats would think he was scared. That would never do. It was easier just to deal with this foolish vole quickly and get back to plundering. He really did love plundering.

So he took the challenge. The vole and the stoat fought.

Scar was many times stronger and more experienced than Richard. Scar picked Richard up and threw him down. Then he did it again. He bit Richard and kicked him and laughed at him.

But Richard did not give up. He kept trying and he kept fighting, even when Scar laughed and mocked and asked him over and over if he gave up; even when Scar admitted that he was a brave little vole and that he had fought well but had never had a chance and there was no shame in giving up and saving his life.

Richard wouldn't give up.

"Well, I can see that you need a lesson teaching to you," cried Scar as he reached down and bit deep into Richard's tail. It was awful for the vole but it gave him a small chance, as it brought Scar's great big ear right down to the level of Richard's mouth. Richard sank his teeth in.

So there they were, the huge stoat biting the vole's tail and the tiny vole biting the stoat's ear. Who would let go first? Richard knew that the whole of vole kind was depending on him. He would not let go. Even when Scar bit right through his tail and most of it came clean off, he still held on to the stoat's ear. He was lifted up and thrown around and twisted and turned in the air but he did not let go.

He hung on and hung on until Scar was exhausted. He held on until Scar could go on no longer and the general of all stoats said:

"I need to rest, you win."

The stoats had to go. They had made the deal, there was no going back. They were beaten. Beaten by a tiny vole with only half a tail.

Richard was a hero of course; a hero with a very small tail. After that voles were born with smaller and smaller tails. Nobody knows exactly why but it reminds us always that one brave vole can change the world." Just then Laura said: "What's that Daddy?" She was pointing over his shoulder.

She had noticed a small stream of water running into the burrow from one of the tunnels.

Voles build their tunnels at an angle, which makes it hard for water to find its way into their homes when it rains, but if the rain is strong enough and goes on for long enough their burrows can be in danger of flooding.

This is the most frightening thing a vole can see. It's more frightening even than the sight of a kestrel or buzzard hovering overhead and looking hungrily down with its sharp eyes.

The burrow is a vole's safe haven. The tunnels are small so that very few dangerous things can get in. The many tunnels mean that even if a predator did find its way in through one tunnel there are many others for the voles to escape from.

Voles keep their burrows well organised so that they feel cosy and warm down there as well as safe. The have comfy areas with little pillows made from straw or grass to relax on. Voles do enjoy relaxing. A vole's burrow is both his home and his castle.

Seeing the water coming into the centre of the burrow Eric and Maura knew that it was time for action. The first thing to be done was to try to stop the water coming in. Each of the voles had to sprint to an entrance and try to block it up with whatever they could. They moved fast and worked hard.

Everyone darted in separate directions. At the very tops of the tunnels they rushed about trying to dam them up and stop the flow of water getting in. Even Jamie completely stopped nibbling and gathered twigs and little pebbles to build a small wall against the flood.

Sara and Anna went to different tunnels to do more work even though they didn't like to be apart - particularly at a time like this.

They all worked in the mud until their paws ached and their

whiskers were dirty and droopy.

They did their best but the water kept coming as the rain kept falling, and all their efforts were in vain. All their little barriers were broken down and broken down and they came to realise that they were not going to be able to stop the burrow from flooding.

"Nature is stronger than anyone," said Maura, "and it is good for a young vole to learn that early on in life I suppose." Maura liked to find a moral in everything that happened so that even if it was a very frightful thing indeed like this, it was not entirely bad.

"Everyone gather quickly by the main tunnel," called Eric.

All the voles, muddy and tired, gathered together. The water was flowing powerfully down into the very centre of the burrow now. The pebbles and mud they had used to try to hold the water back were being carried on the streams of brown water into their home. The level of the water had reached their ankles. They already knew what Eric was about to say, but they still felt tears in their eyes as he told them it was time to leave their home.

They had to leave quickly. Even their store of food had to be completely left behind, a thing not natural to voles. The only things they took with them were their emergency whistles.

Outside it was dark night. It was cold and the rain was beating down relentlessly. It was frightening to feel the great power of nature.

"The thing we must do now is to wait out this storm," called Eric over the howling of the weather. It felt like the wind was grabbing up his words and rushing away with them.

"We need to find a safe place. Somewhere as warm, dry and sheltered as possible. The storm can't last too long and afterwards we will rebuild and make a burrow even better than before. Have heart children, be brave, if we stay together and stay under cover all will be well. Follow me, chins up!"

They searched around under the shrubs, looking for the very best place to hide. They were very careful to be as quiet as possible but they couldn't help making the small shrubs and grass move a little as they trekked through them.

That movement was visible to keen eyes. Nearby in an oak tree, patrolling the large, long, lower branches, a family of owls was on the hunt that night. The local owls had been suffering too in the bad weather. It was hard for them to hunt when it was hard for them to fly and when all the animals they needed to catch were burrowed in underground or hiding safely in their nests. Many owl tummies were rumbling unpleasantly. This group was made up of a mother and her two hungry young ones.

"Tell a story," said Jamie, who was hoping for something to take his mind off the cold and wet, particularly now that he had nothing to snack on.

"Yes please," echoed the other children.

Eric looked to Maura. He was better at telling the scary tales but he knew this was a time for a more comforting kind of story.

"I'll tell you the story of a feast," said Maura, "but not just any feast, this feast was the greatest feast that has ever been enjoyed by any voles anywhere."

All the young voles snuggled together and tried to get as comfy as possible on the damp mud.

"Every vole," continued their mother, "knows how important feasts are. We like nothing better than to celebrate any important or joyful event in our lives with food, family and friends. It's not unusual for us vole folk to spend a whole week or two saving up food to make the most delicious spread for an anniversary, birthday or any other happy occasion. I trust that we will all have many feasts before us in the times to come but none of them could possibly be like the feast I'm about to tell you of. This story concerns a young vole called Esther.

Esther was an unusually bold and brave little thing. In truth, she was too bold and brave. Her poor mother and father were constantly worried because she was forever going off on adventures and taking risks that no sensible vole should ever dream of.

She had a game with herself to see how close she could get to a cat. The aim of this game was to see if she could pluck a hair from the cat's tail.

She was lucky, more than once, to get away with her life and she even lost a small piece of her right ear to a cat's claw!

Her emergency whistle got a lot of use as you can imagine. So much use that it was nearly worn through from all the work it had to do. All the voles in the area were used to having to abandon whatever they were doing or eating to run to her aid when they heard that whistle go.

It was when Esther was out exploring, too far from her burrow as usual, that she came across something most unusual and strange. A Pixie caught in a trap.

You know about traps - they are those horrible metal things that humans make to catch animals like rabbits and hares. They are like a terrible metal mouth, and if an animal steps a paw into one of them it snaps shut on them and holds them fast until the humans come...

What almost never, ever happens though is that a Pixie gets caught in a trap. Pixies are just about big enough to trigger a trap but they are also magical, clever and sharp so that they will almost never end up trapped.

Even a bold little vole like Esther was nervous when she came upon this sight.

The Pixie was muttering to himself: 'You old fool Podocarpus. How did you get yourself caught like this? You've got to keep your feet on the ground, pay attention. Living in your head old man, mind in the clouds. What to do? What to do?' And on he went.

He was a very old looking Pixie. He had a long grey beard and a forehead with deep lines all across it like a freshly ploughed field. He had green eyes which were a little pale, although they had been very bright some hundred or so years ago. Pixies live a very long time.

As Esther watched him from behind some grass she began to feel that there was nothing to fear from this creature. She crept from hiding and keeping low, just in case, she moved towards this Podocarpus."

They heard a flapping sound above them. Maura stopped

telling the story. They all looked up. Birds cast no shadow at nighttime and owls are the most skillful of all nighttime hunters, but the voles saw the shape of a bird above and they heard them calling to one another.

"Everybody down, get close to the ground and stay still," whispered Eric.

Owls are smart and their big eyes are sharp and specially made for seeing at night. They knew that something had moved in that patch of grass and they circled and watched. One of the young birds thought he saw the light of the moon reflected off soft fur and he swooped down. A hooked, black claw hit the ground next to Jamie. As the bird rose, empty-clawed, Jamie let out a little whimper.

The mother owl heard and dived down like lightening. Jamie clung to the ground with all his might but the bird scooped him up into her talons. She flapped her wings and began to rise but that very instant she felt a sharp pain at her ankle.

Looking down she saw two larger voles biting hard into her. She tried to get higher but the voles bit harder and she was forced to release the little one. All three voles fell to the ground. Eric, Maura and Jamie rolled over several times and struggled to their feet.

Now the battle was on. The family of voles took up twigs and darted around trying to defend themselves and confuse the owls. They fought off the owls attacks but they were quickly becoming exhausted and the owls knew they would soon have their dinner.

"Psst," heard Carla. She looked around but saw no one there.

"Psst, over here," from beneath some wet leaves emerged a long nervous nose. "And now you see me," said Sebastian the shrew, "call your family and quickly follow me."

Carla called and everybody ran following the shrew. In a few moments they came to the wall of an old shed made from stone.

"Through here," said Sebastian as he sped into a little gap between the stones. In a moment they were inside, in a dry little stone burrow, safe from the danger outside.

"Make yourselves at home," said Sebastian with a wave of one paw, "it's not much but I live alone and it suits me."

The voles looked around them in relief and surprise. They were in a perfectly round stone chamber in the wall of the old shed. It was warm and dry. There was a rug, woven from grass of three different colours in the centre and even a small fireplace with a little fire burning in a ring of pebbles.

"Make yourselves comfortable. I don't have a lot of food in. After all, I didn't know you would be coming but have a look in my little store here and help yourselves."

The voles didn't want to appear greedy so they all had a very small pawful of food from the store and thanked Sebastian very much.

"Don't mention it," said Sebastian who was enjoying playing the host and the hero.

"I wonder," said Anna and Sara as everyone settled down, "if Mum could finish the story she was telling us before the owls attacked, please."

Maura looked at Sebastian.

"Please do," said the shrew, "I love to hear stories."

So Maura resumed the story after having quickly summarised the story so far, for their host.

"Esther approached the trapped Pixie. He was still talking to himself and he didn't notice the vole until she was right up beside him. When he finally noticed her he leaned over and peered down, examining her closely.

Esther tried to stand as straight and confident as she could. 'Well bless me, a vole of all things,' said Podocarpus, 'you find me in a difficult and dangerous fix little friend as you can observe.'

'I would like to help,' said Esther, 'if I can.'

'The trap is very strong,' said the ancient Pixie. 'I have tried my hardest to open it but it's too tight for me. I'm beginning to fear that I am in quite a deal of trouble. When the humans come to check their traps it will be curtains for me and bad indeed for the Pixie folk here about. After all, we don't want them to know we're here now do we?'

'I hope you don't mind my saying,' Esther replied, 'but aren't Pixies magic? Can't you use your magic to break free?'

'Alas,' came the sad response, 'we are magic, but I have always been more of an expert on levitation and the conjuring of fire, and I find myself unable to make a spell to help myself now. I am growing tired and it gets harder for me to perform any magic at all.'

Esther was very sorry for Podocarpus. A trap is such a terrible thing that all creatures feel sympathy for any other creature hurt in this way. She was determined to help if she could.

She tried to open the jaws of the trap but she didn't have the strength. She pulled and pulled and dangled in the air with all her weight trying to force the trap open even a tiny bit so that he could release his captured leg but nothing worked.

'You are a brave and kind little vole,' said Podocarpus, 'I am most grateful for your efforts.'

But Esther was also a determined vole and she wasn't going to give up just yet. She went and found a very small tree branch which had been blown to the ground. It was a size that meant she could just about drag it over to the trap if she used all her might. When she got it there she managed with much effort to get one end of it into the jaws of the trap near Podocarpus's leg. Then she started to collect any stones she could move. She went back and forth collecting all she could and piled them one by one on the other end of the branch. As she put more and more stones on, that end was pushed down further and further, stronger and stronger and the other end, the end in the trap, was pushed up with some power making the trap start to open little by little.

It took much time and a lot of effort but in the end the trap opened just enough for the Pixie to free himself. He sat on the ground in relief. After a moment or two he looked at the trap, said something under his breath and the trap caught fire and burnt to a cinder in a moment.

Esther nearly jumped out of her fur.

'Fear not my friend,' said the Pixie, 'I simply needed to show that heinous trap who was boss. I would never harm you. I am greatly in your debt. How can I ever repay you? If there is something that I or one of my kind can do to show our appreciation, well I would be most happy.'

With that he gave Esther a little tickle behind her ear.

What an exciting thing for a young vole to hear. Esther thought of all the things the Pixie folk with their magic could do for her. She could have the best burrow and the greatest adventures.

The more she thought however the more she remembered all the trouble she had caused her own folk and how good they had been to her. So she asked Podocarpus for something very special. She asked if it would be possible for the Pixie folk to make a magical feast. The biggest and best feast there had ever been so that she could treat all the voles of the county as a way of saying thank you.

'That is a thing easily done,' said the Pixie, 'a magic feast will be yours with the compliments of the Pixie folk.'

And so it was. Esther invited all the voles from all around to come and it was the greatest and most delicious feast ever. Never have voles or any other animals had such a wondrous spread of delicious foods.

There were nuts and berries and roots and fruits and seemingly endless amounts of the tastiest acorn wines. All the voles ate their fill for a week. Everyone danced and laughed and told stories for a whole seven days. Everybody was very grateful to Esther and she felt very happy. And for a whole week Esther didn't get into any trouble, but only for a week..."

"Bravo," said Eric and Sebastian. The kids all cheered a little cheer.

After the story everyone felt a little better. Sebastian helped them all to get comfy, tucking them into little grass blankets and Maura spoke to the children.

"You see children that we are safe now. We will go back home when the rain stops and rebuild. We will make it as good as new. Remember this when all seems lost: that things will be alright in the end and if it's not alright, it's not the end."

They all curled up and slept for they were very, very tired indeed.

Chapter three- in which the family go on an adventure together

The rain did stop because rain never lasts forever and the voles got to work on repairing their home.

For a whole week after the night of the flood, as the family would come to call it, everyone was quiet and unhappy. Often really shocking things like that leave you shaken for a long time after they have finished.

Then one morning Eric and Maura woke the children early and announced that the whole family was to go on a High Speculation.

"We need a happy adventure to get the juices following again," said Eric, "we need to see and do interesting things to clear the bad memories from our minds. When a vole needs to do this he goes on a special adventure called a High Speculation. This is a long hike with no other purpose than enjoyment and enriching the mind. It is a great vole tradition when the chips are down."

Success in High Speculating takes careful planning. Every adult vole knows this and every young vole learns it. Like most things in a vole's life the most important things in a High Speculation are food and shelter. This means that voles need to learn skill with leaves.

"Leaves," you say, "why leaves?" Well, I'll tell you.

While a leaf might look pretty to you and me and not much more, a vole can see lots of different uses in that same leaf.

When Eric and Maura decided to take the family out on a High

Speculation the first thing they did was ask the children to go out and collect up lots of leaves; oak and sycamore leaves if they could.

All the children collected a small pile of leaves each and brought them back to the burrow. They lined up proudly with their leaves as their parents inspected their work and nodded approvingly to each of them in turn; even Jamie, who had nibbled a hole or two in his leaves.

"On our adventure," Eric spoke firmly, a little like an army officer but with a quick wink to the kids to lighten the mood, "we will need to carry plenty of food with us. We will carry this food in knapsacks, which, we will make from some of the leaves which you have gathered. Take two middle-sized, strong leaves and put them to one side. Yes, those leaves are very good. They will do nicely."

Now Maura gave each of them a very tiny sliver of wood and a blade of grass that had been equally divided by sharp vole teeth into long strings.

"Make a knot with the grass string at the end of your wooden needles," said Eric "and we can start to sew the leaves together to make our knapsacks."

The whole family worked in silent concentration at piecing their leaves together. Laura didn't even notice that she had stuck her tongue out of the side of her mouth; such close, close attention was she paying to her work.

After some time they had all sown their leaves into perfect green pockets. They used some more strings of grass to make straps for their shoulders. They nibbled some more leaves in half and fixed one half on top to keep the rain off the food they would be carrying in them.

In the same way they were able to make hammocks to sleep on and Eric and Maura did the more difficult work of making the pieces that they would be able to use to pitch a tent every night, so that they could sleep safe, sound, warm and dry.

They spent a whole day making all these items and the next day they spent collecting lots and lots of food. Nuts, fruits, berries, bulbs, sweet roots, grass and all types of good things were collected. All this food collecting took another whole day.

That night everyone went to bed early to be well rested for the next day but it was difficult to sleep with the excitement tickling their minds and bubbling in their tummies. All the children were up at dawn poking their parents to wake them up.

Everybody skipped up the tunnel and out into the sunshine. They all stopped for a second and looked up at the blue sky with just a few small white clouds playing in it.

There were still lots of large puddles around and the voles decided to make little boats from leaves and paddle them around with grass paddles. When you are on a High Speculation it is good to do just what takes your fancy.

After a while paddling about they decided they should drop in on Sebastian and ask him if he would like to come along with them.

Sebastian was at his door airing his rug. He was flicking it fast to make any dust and dirt fly out of it. Anna sneezed and Jamie tried to catch some of the flying dust. Every time his paws came near to catching a piece it darted away from him.

"Well now," said Sebastian, "I would love to go with you, it sounds very stimulating indeed but I need to take advantage of this good weather to do some spring cleaning. My poor home got quite damp you know with all that rain."

So the family said good luck and headed off in a line; Eric, Maura, Anna, Sara, Laura, Jamie and Carla, all in a row across the garden and very soon they came to a road.

"Stop," said Maura, "it's time for a talk."

Everyone gathered around and sat down to listen. This was the first time the young ones had been this close to a road.

"This is a road," Maura continued, "roads are made by humans and roads bring humans. They come in massive steel things called cars. They are the most dangerous creatures of all because they kill without knowing or caring. They kill without wanting or needing to eat. They are hard to understand and that makes them more dangerous. So we are even more careful around roads than usual. "

Everyone was taking in this important information and thinking about how big and scary cars were when they heard a loud but shaky voice calling to them. They looked and saw a large and wonderfully coloured bird with an incredible long tail waddling slightly unsteadily towards them. He was big and gold and blue and red, a rainbow of a bird.

"Hello, hello, nice to meet you little animals, nice to meet you," said the large, old male pheasant, for that was what he was, "mice are you?"

Now no one likes to be mistaken for something else but voles get used to this kind of mistake and as they are very proud of how polite they are (more polite than mice by the way), Eric answered in a very pleasant tone of voice.

"We are voles my friend and it is very good to make your acquaintance." Eric liked big words; it felt nice to say them.

"Apologies, my small, new friends. I'm Lord Shaw, but people call me Feathers don't you know, on account of my... well, feathers (and he spread his lovely wings and gave them a shake). What is it you are about this fine day?"

Eric explained that they were out on a High Speculation and then explained what a High Speculation was. Then he explained it all again louder and slower because Feathers was a little deaf due to the large amount of loud bangs he had heard in his life.

He was very impressed with the idea and told the voles how he had spent his youth exploring for something called the Royal Pheasant Society in somewhere he called 'the colonies' which the voles didn't really understand but sounded like a very exciting place indeed.

"Retired now of course," shouted the Lord, "and looking after things here. In fact and on that note and subject, you know I am concerned about what is going on in that field over there, lots of noise and humans coming and going and the smell of pheasants about, don't you know. You won't know what might be going on over there by any chance? I'm really supposed to be informed about these things you know."

The voles looked in the direction Lord Shaw was pointing with his long golden brown wing. They could see that little wooden huts, each with a slanted roof, had been built in rows in a field, but they didn't know of course what was happening there, and they said so to the Lord.

After that they said goodbye and went on their way.

For a short way they had to follow the road. They moved along very carefully. They passed a pothole, a big hole in the road and as they did the children heard their father whisper under his breath, "the Iron Vole."

They had never heard of this Iron Vole before and they all decided to ask about it later when they were somewhere safer. Right then they knew that they should keep moving.

They crossed into a larger, wilder field. They could not see from one end of it to the other and it had lots of trees and rough and thorny plants in it.

Sara saw a little white flash near the bottom of one of the large trees and everyone went to have a look. Over near the tree they found a young rabbit. She was eating a dandelion and clearly really enjoying it. She was nibbling in a circle around the yellow flower faster than the eye could follow. The rabbit didn't notice them until they were very close to her indeed, because she was concentrating so hard on her eating and when she did see them she got a terrible fright. She turned immediately and darted back into her burrow under the tree with another flash of her little white tail.

"This would be a good place to camp for tonight," said Maura. "We can make our tent here and then get our suppers from our knapsacks. "

"And we can hear about The Iron Vole," said Laura, "we all heard Dad mention it when we passed that big hole on the road."

"First we must set up camp," said Maura. All the children got to work helping to build the tent of leaves and unpacking some food. The idea that a good story is coming is a very good way to get a young vole to work hard.

When they were all finished and they were sitting eating in the coziness of their tent (they were safe as well because a little tent made of leaves blends in so well that no predator would know it was there), the kids reminded their parents again about the Iron Vole.

Eric looked a little worried.

"The Iron Vole. That's a very old and scary story. I'm not so sure I should tell you."

"Oh please," all the children pleaded.

"Well, ok. It's a kind of a ghost story but the Iron Vole is not a ghost.

A lot of voles believe that he's real but he's definitely not like you and me. For a start he's big; bigger than you could imagine, big as a big dog, maybe bigger. And he's strong, so strong making holes in the road would be easy for him. Not many have seen him but those who have say he appears in a strong wind when the dust is blown around. The air and the earth mix and there is a burst of fire and the Iron Vole appears - huge and black.

You have to understand that the Iron Vole is not just one story. Different voles tell different stories about him. He seems to have been around as long as we voles ourselves have.
It's not known if he's good, if he's bad, or something else. But

he is terrifying. I can tell you one story about him. This story concerns a vole called Maurice. He was a vole with a problem. Two problems really. First he had an unusually long tail and second his name was Maurice and that rhymes with Mouse. So poor Maurice was called 'Maurice the Mouse'. He didn't like this. He got into fights and arguments and didn't have many friends so he decided one day just to go off on his own and leave all the other voles, and his troubles, behind him.

But very soon he was cold and lonely, lost and even a little hungry. Then things got worse. A dog found him. The dog was big and the dog had a good nose and strong teeth. He found Maurice's scent and came hunting him. Maurice tried to run and he tried to hide but was soon trapped and helpless.

Now Maurice had heard stories of the Iron Vole, so being at his wits end he called out to the Iron Vole to help him. He called out and blew his emergency whistle.

AND THE IRON VOLE CAME.

He came in a storm. He was huge and black with blazing eyes and he chased the dog away. Then he turned to Maurice and Maurice was even more afraid than he had been of the dog. He ran and ran and the Iron Vole chased him. He ran for what seemed to him like hours and he ran for what seemed like miles. His heart beat even faster than his feet were running. He didn't know where he was going or how he hoped to out run the Iron Vole.

He ran all night and still his pursuer was at his heels. After hours of running, as the sun rose in the sky the Iron Vole disappeared. One moment he was there and the next he was gone. Poor Maurice was left exhausted, confused and frightened. He could never make sense of his experience.

In the end, of course, he went home. He told his story. Some believed him, some didn't and Maurice himself could never decide why the Iron Vole chased him. Was it just because he ran? Was this great vole friend or foe...

Now, that's enough story for tonight. It's time to sleep. We can talk more about the Iron Vole another time because it's the kind of story that doesn't end. It will go on as long as there are voles."

They all slept well, tired after their big day. Carla dreamed of the Iron Vole, so big and strong; but was he friend or foe? He was there in her mind forever now.

The next morning they were up early and on the way again after a hearty breakfast.

They had to cross another road. Carla was looking out for any potholes, looking for signs of the Iron Vole.

The next field they came to had the grass all eaten down nearly to the ground. As they crossed it Eric pointed to a group of huge animals standing together in the shade under a big old oak tree. They were red coloured cattle called Red Polls. They have coats of a beautiful warm red colour that looks like you could warm yourself beside it on a cold day.

As they made their way across the field they saw one of the young Red Polls was standing on his own chewing on grass in a sad way with his head down. He had the wonderful bright red coat of his breed but he also had a little shock of blond hair on the top of his head.

Although he was massive compared to a vole or even many

voles put together he didn't seem dangerous. In fact he seemed sad. His great head was held low and his lovely blond mop of hair was flopping down over his huge, dark brown eyes. Laura felt sorry for him at once and she made her way up to him and tried to get his attention. It was difficult for her because she was so small and he was lost in his own sad thoughts.

Laura was not going to give up though so she gulped a gulp, wiped her nose and started to climb up his leg. Then she got to his shoulder and then went up his big, thick neck near to his ear.

"Ahem," she said, "hello there."

The bullock got a bit of a shock when he heard the little voice. He saw the other voles looking up at him and then looked back through his very long eyelashes to see Laura clinging to his coat.

"Ooooh," he said, quite slowly, "what's going on?"

He was clearly a little shocked.

"We're sorry," everyone said loudly. We just wondered why you look so sad and why you're standing over here on your own when all the other cattle are shading themselves and chewing on grass together happily over there under that tree."

"Well, I'm fine I suppose," said the Red Poll, "I'm just a little shy maybe. I just don't find it very easy to talk to people."

"Well you're talking to us," said Laura. "What's your name please?"

"True, but you are all very small and friendly and you did talk to me first. It's not that I actually want to talk that much. I'm happy just to watch and listen most of the time but I don't like people to think I'm quiet or don't ever have anything to say. My name is Andy by the way."

He took quite a long time to say all that because it was the most he had said in a while and he was just getting used to talking to people again. Voles speak quite quickly and it was strange for them to listen to this giant animal talking so slowly.

Just then Carla stepped forward.

"I like your hair," she said.

"Nobody else has hair like this," replied Andy.

"That makes you special Andy," said Carla, "and you don't need to worry about what other people think of you. You can just be yourself and see what happens. Sometimes you can even fly."

"Really, fly?" Andy raised his head.

"Well, maybe not fly all the time but good things happen. You just have to see what happens and not worry."

"Well it has been quite pleasant and easy making friends with you," said Andy, "Perhaps I should worry a little less about these things. After all I have so much more in common with the other cattle, it should be even easier to make friends with them." He blinked his big, brown eyes slowly and brought his neck as near to the ground as he could.

"Climb down," he said to Laura," and thank you all for your

help."

Laura got to the ground and Andy walked over slowly towards the tight knot of Red Poll cattle under the shady tree. The voles watched as he gently nudged his way into the group. He seemed to be getting comfortable there now.

"I don't want you to be getting into the habit of flying you know," Maura said to Carla with a smile and everyone laughed.

That night they set up their tent and their hammocks. All the young ones wanted to hear more about the Iron Vole.

"We can tell stories about meetings with the Iron Vole and they are all interesting in themselves and exciting too but the biggest question is: Who, or what is the Iron Vole?" said Eric. "It's a question no one can answer but aren't those the questions we all want to answer the most? Is he the result of a magic spell gone wrong or out of control? Is he out of control; is there a power behind him? Is he an animal just like us but too big and powerful to understand? Is he a different kind of animal, a kind we know nothing about? Is he an evil spirit or a protecting one? Is he just something we imagine when we are very frightened, a figure from a nightmare, or a dream? Maybe he is the result of folk drinking too much acorn wine eh?"

That night all the young voles talked about the Iron Vole and what they thought he might or might not be. They started to make up their own stories too, which is sign that a young vole is growing up.

The next morning they woke early once more and after packing up all their camping things they went and checked on how Andy the Red Poll was doing.

He was full of news of the new friends he had made and of the things that interest the cattle folk and seemed to have lost a great deal of his shyness. He still spoke in his own quiet, slow voice though and it was very pleasant to listen to when you got used to it.

That was the last day of the voles High Speculation. They took their time on the way home. They talked about the people they had met and the ones they had almost met, as Anna described their brief encounter with the young rabbit. They all agreed that they would go on an adventure like this one again soon.

Before they got back to their own burrow Carla picked some dandelions and brought them to Sebastian the shrew as a souvenir of their trip.

"Oh my," he said when she gave them to him, "exotic treats, how very thoughtful of you. You must all come in and have some dinner with me."

The voles were tired but they enjoyed the evening telling Sebastian of all that happened on their High Speculation. Eric and Maura even shared some acorn wine with the shrew and the children all had plenty of food... And a dandelion petal or two each.

Chapter four- in which the voles go on a rescue mission with Sebastian and Lord Shaw

Everyone was woken that morning by a great noise of shouting and flapping. It was a few days since they had returned from their High Speculation and everyone was enjoying the warm weather, the bad times of the flood forgotten.

Eric decided to see what all the commotion was about. He took his whistle from its hook by the main tunnel and went to discover the source of all the noise and fuss.

Outside he was surprised to see Lord Shaw the pheasant. Eric tried to greet him but the pheasant was far too wrapped up in running about, flapping his wings and talking loudly to himself to notice Eric. The vole had to stand right up on his hind legs and wave his arms, which were not big enough to be very good at being noticed, to get Lord Shaw's attention.

Lord Shaw had been enjoying his morning dust bath when he was disturbed by humans rushing by in cars and trucks. They had gone into the field with the little huts. Lord Shaw followed at a little distance to see what they were up to and just what was worth interrupting his morning wash.

He had waited for the men to move down the line of small wooden structures and then he had crept up to have a peak into the first hut....

Eric finally succeeded in getting that much information out of Lord Shaw. "Just what did you see?" Eric said to Lord Shaw.

"Well, I mean, prisoners, yes prisoners I say, small pheasants in, in cages.."

Eric could see that the old pheasant was very upset and that the situation was serious but by talking gently to him and holding the tip of his wing all the time, Eric was able to coax the story out of Lord Shaw.

After waiting for his chance, Lord Shaw had made his way to the nearest wooden hut. He needed to stretch up onto the tips of his claws to see through a gap in the boards. Inside it was dark and it took a few seconds before the scene became clear to him.

He saw many, many young pheasants - too many to count, all in the dark with hardly enough room to move. Lord Shaw fell right back on his bottom in shock. Could it be true? Pheasants, those noble birds, kept prisoner like this?

He looked into the next hut and the next; they were all the same. All of them were filled with young birds, trapped in the darkness.

After the pheasant had finished his story, Eric thought for only a second, rubbing the end of his chin with his little paw as he always did when considering something really serious and then he reached for his emergency whistle and gave it a long, hard blow. All the voles arrived quickly and even Sebastian came out of his burrow, where he had been rearranging furniture, to see what was going on.

Now Eric was a very small creature and deep down like all voles he was a timid creature but no creature is so small or so timid that they do not recognise when something is wrong and do not feel like putting that wrong thing to rights.

Eric's heart swelled with the feeling that he should do

something, anything he could, about the injustice which Lord Shaw had described, and he explained to the gathered company about the young peasants who were being kept prisoner in the rows of wooden cells in a field not far from where they stood. Everybody agreed that something should be done about this although everybody felt that such a very, very big problem would be hard to solve with a group of creatures as tiny as they were.

"Organisation," said Eric, "organisation and togetherness, that's what we need to bring this rescue mission off successfully. If we work together I believe there is a good chance that we can set these young birds free and put right this terrible wrong." While he spoke though his voice shook just a little. It was clear that he was nervous about the size of the task ahead.

Everybody gave a short cheer but not too big a cheer because they all knew that there was a lot of work still to be done.

That night, while Lord Shaw calmed himself with a cup of extra strong acorn wine, seven voles and one shrew made their way across the garden, carefully across the road, through a hedge and towards the rows of wooden huts. All their hearts were beating extra fast in their chests. Jamie had brought some nibbles along with him to keep his spirits up and Sebastian was singing a little marching song very quietly to help him to stay brave.

"We are shrews on the march cross the fields,
our courage and our hope never yields,
now you see us now you don't, the whole world is our cloak,
we are shrews on the march cross the fields."

Despite the fact that Sebastian was the only shrew present,

everyone found the song up-lifting and joined in with the second verse.

"We are shrews on the march cross the fields, though we are very small indeed,
our hearts are big as houses,
you can ask our friends the mouses,
we are shrews on the march cross the fields."

At this point the voles thought perhaps Sebastian was making it up as he went along but they still joined in.

"We are shrews on the march cross the fields,
where others fear to go a shrew will always lead,
with our friends the voles we heed the call,
we are the bravest of them all,
we are shrews on the march across the fields."

Now they knew he was making it up but he was doing it nicely.

They looked around to make sure that there were no humans in the area. Once they knew it was safe they moved towards the first wooden hut. Each of the huts was locked but a lock is no way to keep a determined vole or shrew out.

Sebastian easily climbed through the small hole that Lord Shaw had peered through earlier on and climbed down the inside until he was on the ground amongst the young pheasants. All the pheasants were milling around, turning in circles and Sebastian had to be very careful to make sure he wasn't trodden on.

He spoke very loudly to try to get their attention.

"Hello," he said, "hello, please listen to me!"

Gradually the young birds realised someone was there and stopped moving around to pay attention.

"I'm here to set you free" said Sebastian.

"Free," said one of the pheasants, "free, what's that?"

"Free," answered Sebastian, "is the best thing in the world. Free means being able to go wherever you want and do whatever you want. Free is the ability to learn all about the world and all the different creatures in it. Free is the ability to make mistakes and to learn from them. Free is feeling the sun on your face and the feeling of lots of space to stretch your wings. Free is the ability to make your own home and make your own family. Free is being able to learn who you are and to be who you are. Free is all those things and free is outside that door."

"Outside the door," said the pheasants, "we've never been outside the door. What's it like out there?"

"Well," Sebastian answered," it's not always good and it's not always safe but there's a whole big world, lots of exciting adventures, there's the wind through your feathers, there's the finding of food, the tasting of different things, there's absolutely everything that you should try."

Well, the young pheasants were very excited by this idea and they all really wanted to get out.

"Right," said Sebastian, "you all just wait there."

He went back out the way he had come in and spoke to the voles.

"I've let everybody in there know what's happening," he said, "and everybody wants to escape. Right now we have to work together."

With that all the voles took up positions, each at the bottom of a plank of wood. They set to work with their sharp little teeth and started gnawing their way through the wood. A lot of it was a little rotten and not very strong and they made short work of it.

Very soon they had made a hole easily big enough for pheasants to come through without even ducking their heads. The first pheasants came through nervously but the ones that followed grew more and more confident.

They stretched their wings and scratched their feet in the dirt and looked all around them at just how big the world was, although in truth they were only looking at one field, and couldn't believe their eyes.

"Ok everyone," said Maura, "all you pheasants are free. You should get out of this field as quickly as you can. Scatter in different directions. The rest of you, Sebastian, all my children, let's get working on the next hut."

Over the next two hours the little rodents worked their way from hut to hut freeing the baby pheasants. They were all very tired but feeling very satisfied too as they were working on the last hut of all. They fields around them were filled with newly released pheasants discovering how good it was to be able to move about as they wanted, dig up their own food, stretch out their wings and necks to their full, long, length and do all the things a pheasant likes to do.

Then the worst happened. They heard the sound of a car turning into the field and saw the blinding beams of its headlights. They gamekeeper had come to check on his birds. As he got out of his car he saw what had happened to his coops. He saw the holes in the sides, he saw that they were empty and he was FURIOUS. He made his way from hut to hut shouting in rage and kicking the walls. He had a large torch in his hand and he was looking for whatever or whoever had caused all this damage.

When his torchlight fell upon a group of little rodents chewing through the last pieces of wood on the last hut and releasing all the young pheasants inside he couldn't believe his eyes.

The pheasants ran in all directions and the gamekeeper made an effort to catch one or two of them but with no success. As he watched the last of them run away he grew even more angry and turned to the small animals who, incredibly, had set them free.

"Why you little...," he shouted and he aimed a kick at them that caught them and sent them flying and then rolling. Then he raised his foot over them and was about to bring his big boot down on them.

Just then, out of nowhere, a strong wind blew up. It lifted the earth with it and swirled it around. There was a flash of fire and out of it appeared a strange and frightening creature. It was large and black and the size of a very big dog. It had fierce glowing eyes.

The gamekeeper took one look at it, forgot about the voles and the shrew and turned tail and ran for his car. He drove away as quickly as he could.

The great creature stood over the voles and the shrew, gazing down on their still forms with its burning eyes. Slowly it reached down and lifted them into its powerful paw.

The next morning Ruth Mullin saw the little pile of creatures outside her kitchen window. She ran outside and peered down at them. They were the voles she had been watching in her garden.

She thought they might be dead and she felt like crying but then she saw a little rise and fall of a chest, a tiny twitch of whiskers.

She knew what she had to do. She ran back into her house and got a warm towel from the hot press. She found one of her mother's shoeboxes and took the shoes out.

She went back outside and scooped the voles up into the towel. They looked like they were asleep now. Their small movements made them look like they were dreaming. They needed help urgently though. It was clear to Ruth that they were hurt.

She carried them home gently and put the towel into the shoebox. She got some oatcakes and crushed them up. She placed a little pile of oat crumbs in the box. She made holes in the lid and put that on. She put the box near a warm radiator. "Good luck little things," she whispered.

That night she couldn't sleep. She kept picturing the tiny creatures, so small and helpless and hoping that they would revive. Of all the animals she liked to watch they were her favourite. They were so small, and nearly everything was trying to catch them for dinner, but they hurried about busy and brave despite it all.

That night all the little creatures dreamed of the Iron Vole. They all saw again the way he had appeared and felt again the power of his presence. It was only Carla though who, even in her dream, wondered if she had done the right thing when, looking up at the sole of the game keeper's big boot about to crash down on them all, she had closed her eyes and wished that the Iron Vole would come and save them.

The next morning Ruth was up before anyone else in the house.

She went straight to the radiator to check on the voles. She lifted the lid of the shoebox slowly and carefully and peeked inside. At first she didn't see the voles. She looked closer and spied a little nose or two. They were hiding in the towel and looking up at her. They seemed to be well recovered from whatever had left them so badly shocked when she had found them. Some of the food she had left in there for them was gone and the towel had been shaped into a new, wave-like shape with folds, in which the little creatures could move about and hide.

Ruth smiled and sighed with relief. She gently carried the box out to the garden, took the lid off and went to watch from the kitchen. She saw seven little voles and something else, a shrew, look at his lovely long nose, climb carefully out of the box. Before they ran off down their holes it seemed like they were hugging each other for a moment but that couldn't be, could it?

"Good little creatures," said Ruth, "I don't know what happened to you but I bet you have some tales to tell."

The vole family and Sebastian had indeed been hugging just as

Ruth thought. They were all still shaken and weak from their ordeal. Sebastian went home and decided to do a second spring clean. The house was really very neat and tidy but he enjoyed doing it.

The voles went to their burrow. They were slow to hang up their emergency whistles on the pegs by the main tunnel.

"Come on now," said Maura, "let's get some food together and have a nice meal."

That's just what they did.

Later when they had all had their fill and were starting to feel a little better Eric said:

"Well, that's probably enough adventure for a little while."

Everyone heartily agreed.

"Maybe we should think about planning another one sometime soon though."

Printed by Amazon Italia Logistica S.r.l.
Torrazza Piemonte (TO), Italy